Who's a Big Bully Then?

Michael Morpurgo

Who's a Big Bully Then?

With illustrations by
Joanna Carey

Barrington Stoke

To all the children who read this book

First published in 2004 in Great Britain by
Barrington Stoke Ltd
18 Walker Street, Edinburgh, EH3 7LP

www.barringtonstoke.co.uk

This edition first published 2017

4u2read edition based on *Who's a Big Bully Then?*
published by Barrington Stoke in 2000

A CIP catalogue record for this book is available
from the British Library upon request

ISBN: 978-1-78112-763-6

Printed in China by Leo

Contents

Chapter 1
Darren Bishop

It all began with Darren Bishop. Every problem I have at school always begins with Darren Bishop. He's been getting at me all year, ever since I first came to this school. Darren Bishop is very big. He has a big neck, big arms and a big head. He has the biggest head in the whole school, and I hate him.

I'm also scared of him, so I do my best to keep out of his way. But in the end, I always bump into him.

Some days I even bunk off school so as not to meet him. I'm so scared of him. I don't know why he picks on me. Maybe it's because I'm small and skinny. Anyway, he does all he can to mess up my life.

He calls me bad names like 'chicken', 'little git' and 'baby face'. And he doesn't just call me names. He makes horrible faces at me. He flicks out my tie and pushes me around.

But I stay cool, even when he kicks my bag and stamps all over my books.

I don't stay cool because I'm brave. I know he just wants me to have a go at him, so that he can beat me up. But I'm not stupid. Nothing he does is ever going to make me fight him.

Last week I had the good luck to get my own back.

Chapter 2
Sports Day

It was Sports Day. I've never been any good at ball games like football. I just get pushed around all the time. But running, that's something I can do. So I was looking forward to Sports Day.

I do best in the 200 metres. It had been easy for me to get into the final. There were eight of us in the line, just waiting for the starting gun. Beside me, in the next lane, was big Darren Bishop. This was my chance to show him up, and I was going to take it.

My dad had come to see me run. He doesn't come into school often. He's always too busy on the farm. But he always comes to Sports Day. And I know why. He loves to see me win.

He was a fast runner himself when he was a kid. Or so he tells me. "That's where you get it from," he says to me.

There Dad was, in the crowd. He was very excited. (Mum won't come because he jumps up and down and shouts and she hates that.)

"Go on, son," Dad shouted. "You can do it. Don't look behind you. Get those legs working."

I waved at him, hoping to shut him up. I did want him there. But he shouts so loudly that people stare and grin and I hate that.

Darren Bishop had seen him and was grinning.

"What a nerd your dad is!" he said loudly so everyone could hear. "Is he drunk or something?"

I was really angry, but I looked the other way and said nothing. But Darren just went on at me.

"What's it like to have a little git for a dad?" he went on. "And your mum's a little git too, isn't she?"

That was too much. I turned on him like an angry dog. If he wanted a fight, then he could have one, right now. It was only the starting gun that saved me.

Bang! We were off. I was all fired up, but not to win. I didn't care about winning any more. All I wanted to do was to beat big Darren Bishop. I just wanted to beat him in front of everyone.

He rushed off fast. He was soon miles in front of me. But I knew he'd gone off too fast. I hung back and just let him think he was winning. He'd soon be out of puff.

The crowd was going wild. They could see that I was passing all the other runners and coming up behind Darren. But Darren couldn't see me. I was running faster and faster. Now there was only Darren left in front of me.

Then I was beside Darren, and he was beginning to slow down. He looked across at me and I saw in his eyes that he knew he was beaten.

"You don't look so good," I said. "Are you feeling OK? There's a long way to go yet for a big lump like you." And I just raced past him and away, waving to him as I went.

"I'll get you, you little git," he yelled at me. "I'll get you."

"Byee," I shouted back at him. "Byee."

I was having a lot of fun. I had never run so fast. My legs just seemed to fly over the ground. I was near the finish. I had a quick look behind me. Darren Bishop looked as if he was going backwards! I raced towards the tape. The crowd was jumping up and down.

And my dad was yelling and running out onto the track to wave me on. I put my arms up as I ran and felt the tape against my chest. I had won. It was the best moment of my life.

I looked back. There was Darren Bishop, puffing and panting as he came up to the finish. His face was bright red. I had beaten him in front of the whole school and it felt great.

I had a great crowd round me. Mr Griffiths, the Head, came up to me and shook my hand.

"Well done," he said. "Go on like that and you'll be in the Olympics one day."

My proud father was standing there, grinning. Everyone was hitting me on the back and telling me how well I'd done. No, not quite everyone. I didn't see Darren Bishop after the race. He just went off somewhere.

I was loving all the fuss and the gold medal I got. But I couldn't forget Darren's horrible words.

"I'll get you," he'd said. "I'll get you."

I didn't know when, I didn't know where, but I knew that sooner or later he'd come after me.

It was sooner, not later, that he came.

Chapter 3
The Plan

It was in morning break the next Monday. I saw Darren coming towards me across the playground. He had his horrible gang with him. I looked around. There was nowhere to run to. I was trapped.

I tried to look as if I wasn't scared. But I was. I was really scared. This was it. I was going to get it now.

"Your time's up, baby face," Darren said. He pushed me against the wall and thrust his face close to mine. "I've come to get you, just like I said. You know what you are? You're chicken. You're scared, aren't you?" And he pushed me again.

"No, I'm not," I said, trying to sound brave.

"Fight!" someone yelled. "Fight!"

By now we seemed to have the whole school round us.

"OK," I went on, "if it's a fight you want ..." I was trying to think of a way out, any way out.

Darren grabbed me by the tie and pulled me towards him.

"I'm going to mash you to pulp, and I'm going to enjoy every moment of it. I'm a bully, a big bully. I'm the biggest bully in the school and I like it. Do you know why? Because I get to beat up little gits like you."

That was the funny thing. It was when Darren bragged that he was a bully that I had my idea, my ace idea.

"All right, I'll fight you," I said, "but not here. What's the point? No fun for anyone, is it? I mean, everyone knows you'd win."

Darren Bishop didn't know what I was talking about. And he didn't know what to do next. He took a long time to think about it.

"You called me chicken, right?" I went on.

"No," said Darren. "I didn't just call you chicken. I said you were scared too." And he hit me hard in the chest.

"What about you?" I said. "Aren't you ever scared? I mean, we're all scared of something. Everyone is."

"Well, I'm not," Darren replied. "I'm not scared of anything."

"Are you sure?" I asked.

"Yeah, baby face, quite sure. Just you try me."

Great. Darren Bishop had fallen right into my trap.

"OK," I said. "You know Mr Langdon's farm, where those big sheds are? It's just outside town, beyond the football ground. I'll meet you there at six o'clock tomorrow morning. There'll be no one about."

"What for?" Darren asked. I could tell he was unhappy.

"For a dare. So we can find out who's chicken, you or me."

"What if it's all a trick?" Darren said. He didn't like my idea. He was trying to get out of it. But I was going to keep him to it. "What if you're not there?" he said.

"Oh, I'll be there," I told him. "And if I'm not, then you can mash me into pulp some other time, can't you? OK?"

Chapter 4
Dawn

So we'd set up a plan. We'd all meet at Mr Langdon's farm at six o'clock the next morning. Just the right time for a dare.

I live quite close to Mr Langdon's farm. My dad works there. He's always worked there. He does all sorts of jobs. He looks after the sheep and feeds the pigs. He makes the hay, harvests the corn and looks after the cows.

I grew up on the farm and, just like my dad, I love the cows best of all. OK, so they are a bit messy. So what?

If you have cows you have to have a bull. We've got a bull, a huge reddy-brown bull with long and pointed horns.

He's called Olly. He's a bit old now. He's nice and gentle – he always has been. I've known him just about all my life. Olly's so gentle that my dad even let me sit on his back when I was little.

Darren Bishop was a town boy, like almost everyone in my school. He didn't know anything about bulls. He thought that all bulls chase you, and most of all if you're wearing red. He had no idea that Olly, though he looked scary, was in fact as gentle as a lamb.

I knew he'd be scared of Olly. This made me grin. My plan was perfect.

The next morning was misty and cold. I crept out of the house and ran down the lane. There were about 20 boys waiting there. They had propped their bikes up against the farm shed. Darren was there and he snorted at me.

“Well, baby face.” He grinned. “What’s this dare of yours, then?”

“You’ll see,” I told him. “It’s this way, not far.”

*

I got over the fence into the field, and they came after me. We walked a long way. The mist was getting thicker and thicker. They kept on asking me where we were going. I only said, "You'll see."

At the next gate I stopped and waited until they were all there. Then I spoke in a hushed voice. “He’s in here,” I said.

“Who is?” Darren asked. “And why are you speaking so softly?”

“Sssh!” I said. “He doesn’t like a lot of noise. It makes him angry. And we don’t want him angry, do we?”

“Who?” Darren yelled. *He* was angry now.

"The bull," I said, so everyone could hear. "There's a big bull with horns, *big* horns, in this field. He's out there somewhere in all that mist. I'm going to find him and I'm going to catch him. I'm going to lead him round the field by the horn. Then you're going to do the same. OK? That's the dare. You're not scared, are you?"

There was a very long silence. Then Darren spoke. "Course not," he said, in a low voice.

But when I opened the gate to go into the field, no one wanted to come with me.

"Come on," I said. "You won't be able to see anything if you don't come in."

They came just inside the gate, and stopped there. So I went out into the misty field alone.

"Where are you?" I called out. "Where are you? Who's a big bully then? Who's a big bully?"

I didn't have too long to wait. I could hear the thunder of the bull's hooves. The ground shook.

And then he came charging out of the mist towards me, tossing his head and snorting. It was great, better than I could have hoped for. He looked just like a mean, angry bull. But I knew my Olly. He soon slowed down to a walk. Then he stopped and looked at me out of his wild, wide eyes.

"Who's a big bully then?" I said loudly, so they could all hear how brave I was.

Olly began to paw the ground. He lowered his head at me and tossed his horns in play. I knew it was in play, but the boys didn't. I waved at Darren and the others. He was on the other side of the gate now. They all were.

"It's OK," I called out. "He's a nice bully. Look at this."

Then I walked right up to Olly and patted his neck. I rubbed him between his horns where I knew he liked it. He stood quite still and snorted at me, as he always did when he was pleased to see me. Some cows came up out of the mist, mooing for him. Olly lifted his head and roared back at them. It was a scary roar.

“Now, Olly,” I said softly, “you see those boys by the gate. They think you’re a mean bull, a real killer. That’s what I want them to go on thinking. So don’t look soft, OK? Look angry, Olly. Can you do that for me? I want you to scare them silly.”

And Olly tossed his head again and swished his tail. Then I had the coolest idea I’d ever had. I took off my coat and began to flap it at him, like they do in a bull fight.

Olly snorted at me angrily. He lifted his head and showed me the whites of his eyes. I'd never seen him look so mean. He was playing his part so well. Then I knelt down in front of him and shook my coat at him. Olly pawed the ground, kicking up great chunks of earth.

"Well done, Olly," I said in a soft voice. "That's great, just great. Now I'm going to take you over to meet them. Look angry, OK? I want you to look *mean*, really mean."

I got up, took Olly by the horn and led him slowly towards the gate. Big Darren Bishop and the others were already backing away, staring at us as we came. Darren had gone quite white.

"Your turn now, Darren," I said, as I opened the gate. "Come on in. It's easy. Honest it is."

Darren ran. They all ran. They rushed off into the mist and left me alone with Olly.

I smiled and smiled. I just couldn't stop smiling. I put my arms around Olly's neck and thanked him.

"You're the best bull in the world, Olly," I said. "Who's a big bully boy?" And I smiled all over again.

Chapter 5
Who's a Big Bully Then?

I ran all the way home. I was longing to tell my parents about how I'd tricked big Darren Bishop. They were having breakfast. They didn't look at all happy.

"Where have you been?" my dad asked. "We've been looking for you everywhere."

"I've been so worried," said my mum. "How often have I told you not to go off like that without telling us?"

"Well?" my dad went on. "What *have* you been doing then?"

"Let him have his breakfast first," my mum said, "or he'll be late for school."

As I ate my breakfast, I told them the whole story. After a bit I saw that my dad was looking at me in an odd way. My mum had gone very pale. They kept looking at each other as I told them what I'd been doing with Olly.

"I knelt down right in front of him like in a proper bull fight. I flapped my coat at him. He was great. You should have seen him, Dad. He was pawing the ground and ..."

"You did *what*?" my dad yelled. "You did *what*?"

"I was just playing, Dad. Then I just took him by the horn and walked him across the field. I wish you could have seen me, Mum.

Olly was great. Gentle as a lamb. Darren and his lot, they all thought he was a real killer bull."

My mum had her head in her hands.

"What's the matter?" I asked.

"What's the matter?" My dad sounded upset, really upset. "I'll tell you what's the matter. That bull you led round the field by the horn, that bull wasn't Olly. I put Olly into the shed two days ago. He's got a bad foot. So Mr Weldon let us have his bull to be with the cows. And Mr Weldon's bull is just about the meanest, most wicked bull I have ever met. That's what's the matter."

I didn't want to eat my breakfast after that. I just wanted to be sick.

I didn't want to go to school at all. I said I felt too sick – but my parents made me. By the time I got there, the story was all round the school – how I had knelt down in front of an angry, mean bull and how big Darren Bishop had run off. I was the hero of the hour and top of the pops.

Darren Bishop didn't dare show his face. He stayed off school.

It should have been the happiest day of my life, but it wasn't. I felt far too sick to enjoy a moment of it.

A Letter from the Author

Nethercott House
Iddesleigh
Winkleigh
Devon
EX9 8BG

Dear Reader,

Shall I tell you something? That was a true story. Not the part about the school bully, but the bit at the end ...

Many years ago, I went into a field on the farm where I live in Devon. I walked up to the bull in there and patted him. I knew he was gentle. (I still felt very brave.)

That evening the farmer said to me when I met him in the lane, "Be careful if you go into the field where the bull is. He's a new one, he only came yesterday. He can be a bit mean."

To me the bulls had looked just the same!

I didn't feel brave any longer. Funny how you can be scared after it's all over.

*

Maybe I should tell you a bit about the farm where I live.

Most farms have cows or sheep or pigs or hens or geese or ducks. Our farm does too. But our farm has children too, 1,000 of them every year. (Not all at once!) They don't come just for a walk round. They come for a whole week to help run the farm. They are the farm workers! Just so long as it's safe, the children do it. (They don't go into the field with a bull, for example!)

And it's a *real* farm, not a play farm where you come to cuddle a lamb and stroke a horse, though they do that too.

It's a huge farm too. It's about as big as 250 football pitches. There are 80 milking cows, 500 sheep, 40 pigs, 100 beef cattle, 50 calves, 35 ducks, 42 hens, 3 geese, 3 donkeys, a horse and a whole lot of farm cats and dogs.

The teachers and children who come here stay for a week.

There's a playroom (we call it the "noisy room") with ping-pong and table football. There's a classroom and a sitting room with lots of books.

Outside there's a big field to run around in, with cow-pats for goal posts. Nice and messy!

*

This is what the children do every day.

7 a.m. Get up. Have a cup of tea. Go out on the farm in three groups (12 in each). One group goes to milk the cows. Another goes to feed the pigs and calves. Another feeds the horse and donkeys, and opens up the hens and ducks and geese. Back for breakfast.

9.30 a.m. Out onto the farm again, one group brushes down the dairy. Another feeds or moves the sheep. Another puts the horse and donkeys out. Another cleans out the stables and feeds the hens and ducks and geese.

11 a.m. Time for a break and a drink and a biscuit. (We need it!)

After our break, it's work in the classroom, or it's playtime.

After lunch, we go out to work on the farm again in our three groups. What we do depends on the time of year and the weather.

We clean out sheds (lots of these), bring in logs for the fires, pick up apples and potatoes (at harvest time), pick raspberries, strawberries in the walled garden or look for blackberries in the hedges. We help with the corn harvest. There is always something that needs to be done.

We have three good hot meals a day. (I don't do the cooking, which is lucky for the children!) Supper is at 5 p.m. Then at 6 p.m. off we go again.

The groups change jobs so everyone gets a turn. The cows have to be milked, the pigs and calves have to be fed, the horse and donkeys have to be fetched in from the field. The eggs must be collected and the hens and ducks and geese have to be shut up for the night, in case the fox comes. And he does come all too often.

We come back to the house at 7.30 p.m. for a hot chocolate and a story. I go up once a week to read them a story. And one of the ones I like best is *Who's a Big Bully Then?*

If you or your teacher or your mum or dad would like to know more about the farm visits – we call it Farms for City Children – then you can write to me, Michael Morpurgo, at:

Nethercott House
Iddesleigh
Winkleigh
Devon
EX9 8BG

Farms for City Children is a charity with three such farms – one in Wales, one in Gloucestershire and one here in Devon. We now welcome over 3,000 primary school children from our towns and cities ever year.

Maybe your school would like to come too. I hope so.

All the best,

Michael Morpurgo

Our books are tested
for children and young people by
children and young people.

Thanks to everyone who consulted on
a manuscript for their time and effort in
helping us to make our books better
for our readers.